BIG and LITTLE at Home

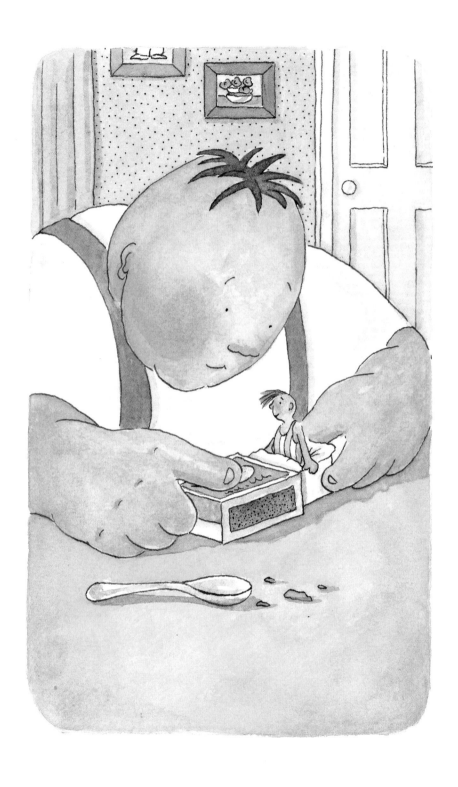

BIG and LITTLE at Home

Sue Limb

Pictures by
Siobhan Dodds

ORCHARD
BOOKS
LONDON

For Emily

FIRST STORYBOOKS

Big and Little
Sue Limb
Pictures by Siobhan Dodds

Mr Loopy and Mrs Snoopy
Sue Limb
Pictures by Keith Brumpton

**Mary, the Witch and
the Ten Little Brothers and Sisters**
Cathy Lesurf
Pictures by John Bendall

Text copyright © Sue Limb 1989
Illustrations copyright © Siobhan Dodds 1989
First published in Great Britain in 1989 by
ORCHARD BOOKS
96 Leonard Street, London EC2A 4RH
Orchard Books Australia
14 Mars Road, Lane Cove NSW 2066
1 85213 141 1
Printed in Belgium

CONTENTS

Chapter One

BIG BAKES A CAKE

Big and Little lived in a house by the sea. Big was so very large that if he came to your house, his head would nearly touch the ceiling. And Little was so small that he lived down the plughole in Big's bath. They were the best of friends, and this was their song:

> My name is Little
> And Big's my name
> If there's ever any trouble
> We're the ones to blame
> We like having picnics
> In the garden and the bath
> And do we have a good time?
> Do we?—Not 'arf!

One day Big and Little had got up late. So they were having their breakfast at lunch time. Big had bought a new breakfast cereal.

"I'm looking forward to this," he said. "It says on the packet it's full of golden goodness and crunchy crackleness and it's made with sugar and honey and all things nice. And when you pour milk on it, it makes the best noise ever."

So Big poured the milk on.

BANG POP CRICKLE-CRACKLE-CRICKLE
BANG BANG BANG
POPO POOP PPPOOOPPP
WHIZZZ WHIZZ WHIZZ
BANG BANG BANG

Little ducked down and hid behind an eggcup.

"Good gracious!" he said. "It's deafening! What a racket! It's worse than a cowboy film. My nerves are in shreds! You know how delicate I always feel first thing in the morning! It's terrible!"

Big was munching his way through the first mouthful.

"It tastes terrible, too," he said. "Ugh! Horrible! Much too sweet! It's makin' all my teeth jump!"

"It's all that sugar and honey," said Little. "I keep telling you you should cut down on sweet things. No

wonder it takes me half an hour to walk around you. You ought to eat apples instead, and keep yourself in trim. I'm very very trim."

And he did a few pirouettes on the breadboard just to show off how slim he was. But Big wasn't interested.

"Ugh!" he said. "I think I'll have to have something else—to take away the taste of that horrible cereal."

So Big had bread and jam and ginger nuts and chocolate biscuits and apples and bananas.

"There you are!" he said to Little. "I did have three apples—see?"

"Hasn't the nasty taste gone away yet?" asked Little suspiciously.

"Not quite," said Big. "Nearly, though. I think I'll just have another sixteen marmalade sandwiches. That should do the trick."

But when Big had finished his marmalade sandwiches, the nasty taste had still not gone.

"It's no good," said Big, "I'll have to have some cake. This is an emergency."

"But you've eaten all the cake!" said Little.

"Then I'll just have to go out and buy some more," said Big.

"You can't! It's lunchtime. All the shops are closed."

"Bother!" grumbled Big. "I'll have to make a cake, then." Big hadn't made a cake before, but he didn't tell Little that. He tried to look quite expert and relaxed, and he whistled as he worked.

He got an enormous mixing bowl and put thirty-six eggs in it, and then fifteen pounds of flour and seven pounds of sugar. Then he stirred it with a huge spoon.

"You're making a terrible mess with that cake," said Little, edging backwards away from the mixing bowl. "I don't want dollops of nasty sticky goo all over my nice new shoes."

So Little climbed up onto a shelf to get out of the way. Big *was* making a mess. The table was already covered with sticky cake mixture and he'd only just started.

11

"Oh dear," said Big. "What comes next? Eggs, flour, sugar ... I wish I could remember. I wish I had a cookbook. I must try and have a think. I hate thinking. It always gives me a pain in the head. Errr ... er ... no, it's no use. Maybe I should put some tomato sauce in. And a bit of pickle."

"Tomato sauce and pickle! In a cake?" cried Little. "Whatever next? Don't forget the pork sausages! Hee hee hee!" And Little laughed so hard, he fell off the shelf—right into the cake mixture!

"HELP!" he cried, quite loudly for such a small person. "Help! Nasty, sticky—ugh! Big! Help me! I'm drowning in horrible muck! Yeargh! Get me out! Help me, Big!"

"Dear, oh dear," said Big with a secret smile. "Poor old Little. Fallen in the cake mix. Here you are then."

And Big pulled him out, and held him up and stared.

"I've never seen such a mess," said Big. "I'll have to put you under the tap to get you clean."

So Big turned the tap on and held Little under it until he was quite clean.

"Help!" shouted Little, struggling as the water ran down his neck. "Help! This water's cold! Stop it, Big! UGH!"

"Dear me!" said Big. "I'm very sorry. I didn't notice

that, Little. I'm sorry. Though they do say cold showers help to keep you in trim. I'll just turn on the other tap."

So Big turned on the hot tap. And he rubbed Little all over with soap.

"Eeeeeeeh! Stop it!" giggled Little. "That tickles! And hey! Help! This water's much too hot! And oooooo! Ugh! I've got soapsuds in my mouth!"

And Little spat them out as hard as he could.

"Funny," remarked Big. "I thought spitting was bad manners. But your Auntie Gertrude taught you the very best manners, you said."

"All right, all right!" said Little. "Joke's over! Now put me by the fire to dry. And if I get a cold, it'll all be your fault."

"You'll be all right, Little," said Big. "You'll soon be dry. I'll play my whistle and you can dance. Then you'll dry off quicker."

And that's exactly what they did.

Chapter Two

LITTLE HAS A COLD

Next day, Little didn't come up the plughole as usual to visit Big. Big was anxious.

"Oh dear!" he said to himself. "That's a bit odd." The next day came, and still Little didn't appear.

"Crumbs!" thought Big. "I wonder what's happened to him? I hope he's all right."

On the third day, Big was really worried. He ran into the bathroom and shouted down the plughole.

"Little! Hey, Little! Are you all right? Are you coming up to play today? .... Little?"

Then Big heard a faint faraway sound. It was Little singing his song—but it didn't sound at all like it usually did.

"My dabe is Little
I live dowd the plughole
If you cadn't hear me
Clead out your lughole!
I've beed livig dowd here
For years and years
If you cadn't hear me
Thed clead out your ears!"

Big scratched his head.

"Little!" he called. "Is that you? You sound all funny. Are you coming up, Little?"

There was no answer, but Big could hear a tiny coughing sound, getting nearer and nearer.

"I'b comig! I'b comig! cough-cough-cough!"

And then up Little popped—out of the plughole. But he didn't look his normal perky self.

"Little!" said Big. "What's the matter?"

"Atishoo!" went Little. "Can't you see what's the batter? I've got a terrible cold, that's what. Cough-cough-cough."

"Oh dear," said Big. "I'm ever so sorry. What can I do to make you feel better? Shall I play my whistle for you to dance? Would that be a help?"

"I can hardly walk, let alone dance, you stupid great pudding!" snapped Little.

"Oh dear, oh dear," said Big. "Would you like something to eat? How about a nice peanut?"

"*Must* you talk about food all the time? I couldn't even look a peanut in the face," groaned Little. "ATISHOO! All I want is to go to bed."

Suddenly Big had a really good idea. He jumped in the air and gave a great twitch.

"Ooooh help! Crumbs!" he cried. "I think that must have been an idea! They always make me jump."

Big ran into the kitchen and emptied all the matches out of a matchbox. Then he folded up one of his clean handkerchiefs and tucked it in all round, till it was a nice, soft, cosy little bed.

18

"Here you are, Little," said Big. "I made a bed for you." Little sneezed twice and crawled into the bed. He pulled up the handkerchief and snuggled down in the matchbox. It was really very comfortable.

For two days Big took care of Little. He brought him spoonsful of hot milk to drink, and a carefully buttered cornflake to try and tempt Little to eat.

"How are you feelin' today, Little?" he asked on the third day.

"Atishoo!" went Little. "Awful! If only I could remember my Auntie Gertrude's cold cure. It's magic. It never fails."

Just then something strange happened to Big. His eyes looked from left to right.

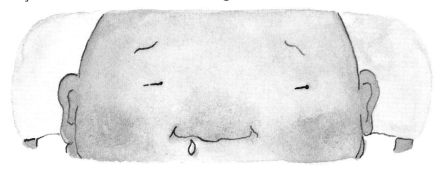

"AAAAAAAAAAAAAAAAAAAAAAAAAAAH—
AAAAAAAAAAAAAH—" went Big. He stood still,
and closed his eyes . . .

"AAAAAAAAAAAAAAAAAAAAAAAHHHHHH—
AAAAAAAAAAHHHHHHHHHHHHHHHHHHH—"
He opened his mouth very wide . . .

"aaaaaaaaAAAAAAAAAAAAAAAAAAAATISH-
OOOOOOOOOOOOOOOOOOOOOOO!!!!!!!" Big's
sneeze was so big, it blew a pile of washing-up over.

"Stop!" cried Little. "Stop! Don't sneeze any more!
You'll wreck everything. Hold your nose tight. Then
you won't sneeze."

"All right," said Big. "I'b holdig it."

Then suddenly Little jumped up in the air and
clapped his hands.

"I've remembered my Auntie Gertrude's cold
cure!" he cried. "It goes like this:

ATISHOO ATISHOO COUGH COUGH COUGH
I won't have this nasty cold: I'll throw it right off!
SNIVEL AND SNIFFLE SNEEZE AND WHEEZE
AND BLOW
I don't want you up my nose so
OFF YOU GO!

Now hold your nose tight and turn round three times
with your eyes shut."

So Big held his nose very tight and turned round
three times with his eyes shut. And so did Little.

"It's worked!" said Little. "My cold's gone! I feel
better! How are you, Big?"

"Ooooooh, well—I feel a bit giddy from all that
turning round."

"Yes, but what about your *cold?*" asked Little.

"Oh yes!" said Big in surprise. "It's gone! Your

auntie must be ever so clever, Little. I feel like playing my whistle now. Do you want to dance?"

"First I'll sing my song," said Little. "I can sing it properly now, because my nose isn't blocked any more.

"My name is Little
I live down the plughole
If you can't hear me
Clean out your lughole.
I've been living down there
For years and years
If you can't hear me
Clean out your ears!"

Then Big played his whistle and Little danced, to celebrate getting better from their colds. And Big was very happy, because it would soon be teatime.

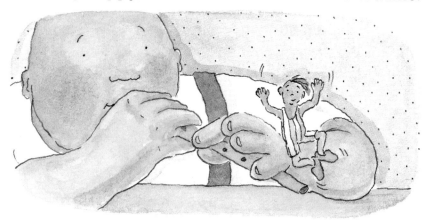

Chapter Three

BIG AND LITTLE
SOW SOME SEEDS

One day, Big and Little had finished their breakfast.
Big did the washing up while Little sat in an eggcup
and watched. And while Big washed up, he sang his
song:

"My name is Big
I live by the sea
I like my breakfast
And dinner and tea
I like eating crisps
And orange to drink
And fish fingers too
And jelly that's pink
And porridge and toast
And cakes without end
But oh! What I really like best
Is my friend."

23

When Big had finished the washing up he threw some crumbs out to the birds. The sun was shining and the sky was a bright, fresh blue.

"Can we go out into the garden, Big?" asked Little. "I've never seen your garden before."

"'Course we can," said Big. "It's springtime now. So we won't have to put our coats and hats on. Good job too. Takes me ages."

So together they stepped out into the sunshine. Big took some deep breaths and swung his arms about. Then he jumped up and down on the spot.

"Steady on!" said Little. "It may be springtime but you mustn't get too excited, Big. You wouldn't want to knock the shed over, now would you?"

Big looked around. He liked his garden. He liked its look and he liked its smell.

"What do you think of it, Little?" he asked.

"Hmmmmm," said Little doubtfully, "it's a bit boring, isn't it? I mean, it's all just bare earth. Nothing growing. No plants."

"Oh crumbs!" said Big. "Breadcrumbs and cake-crumbs and gingerbiscuit crumbs! I forgot to sow the seeds!"

"Honestly!" said Little. "You'd forget your name if it wasn't short."

"My name isn't short," said Big. "It's Big."

Big went into the garden shed and looked around for the seed packets. There were lots of old spades and forks and rakes in there, all mixed up together with sacks and bags of old potting compost and

hundreds and hundreds of plant pots. But in the end Big found what he was looking for. They were tucked away in an old saucepan: his seed packets. He took them out to where Little was sitting on the wall.

"It's not too late to sow the seeds now," said Big. "Let's sow them today."

"All right," agreed Little. "What have you got?"

"Oh—beans and peas and tomatoes and spinach and onions and radishes and—"

"What?" cried Little in dismay. "All boring old vegetables? Honestly, Big, you never think about anything except food! What about a few lovely flowers? You want a bit of colour and perfume. You want to come out here on a summer's evening and go, 'Mmmmmmmmmnnnn, heavenly!' Not fall over a row of pongy old turnips!"

Big thought for a while. He'd never really bothered much with flowers. He usually just grew things to eat. In fact Big had often wished there were chocolate cake trees and sausage roll bushes as well as tomatoes and carrots and peas. But he knew how sensitive and particular Little was. And he was quite willing to give flowers a try if that was what Little wanted. After all, Little was so very small. Almost as small as a bee. And bees liked flowers, didn't they? So it was only natural.

"I'll tell you what, Little," said Big. "You go and sow some flower seeds at the bottom of the garden, and I'll sow some vegetable seeds up here."

So Little took a handful of flower seeds (Big had bought a couple of packets by mistake) and off he went down to the far end of the garden. He hadn't

been there long when there was a sudden, very loud
CHEEEEEEEEP!
and a sparrow bounced up to him. Little was
terrified. A sparrow may only seem a small bird, but
to Little she looked very big indeed.

"Oooh!" screamed Little. "What an enormous bird!
Don't eat me! I don't taste very nice! Go away!"

And Little hid behind a dandelion leaf. But the bird
saw him and hopped up close. She wanted to get a
good look. She'd never seen a small creature quite
like him, before.

"CHEEEEEEEEEEEP!" she said.

"Don't eat me!" pleaded Little. "Why don't you eat
some of those crumbs Big put down for you? But

28

please don't eat me! I taste horrible, really I do! I can't even bear to suck my own thumb!"

Just then Big saw what was happening.

"Hey, Little!" he called. "She doesn't want to eat you! She's only after the seeds! Throw her the seeds!"

Little threw the seeds to the bird straight away. She pecked them up hungrily. Little watched from

behind the dandelion leaf. He was still a bit scared. The bird's eyes were so very bright and her beak looked so very sharp. Little was glad he wasn't a flower seed.

"You see, Little," said Big, coming up to watch. "Even birds need their breakfast. And that reminds me—I'm getting peckish! Ho ho!"

"Yes," said Little. "It's ten minutes since you had your breakfast. You must be starving."

Big picked Little up very gently and carried him indoors. He put him down on the table.

"Time for elevenses," said Big.

"It can't be!" said Little. "It's only ten o'clock!"

"Time for tenses, then," said Big. "Lets have crisps and orange juice and apples—I'm on a diet."

They carried the crisps and orange juice and apples out into the garden and sat down on the grass to have their tenses. Big threw a few crisp crumbs to the birds. And Little gave his sparrow a snack. Then Big felt so happy that he burst into song:

30

My name is Big
I live by the sea
I like my elevenses
Tenses and tea
I like eating crisps
And jelly that's pink
And fish fingers too
And orange to drink
And porridge and toast
And cakes without end
But oh! what I really like best
Is my friend.

After they had had their tenses, Big played his whistle to the birds, and they all joined in. And Little dozed in the sunshine on a most comfortable daisy leaf. They were both looking forward to the summer, when the seeds would grow, and Big and Little knew they would have lots more adventures.